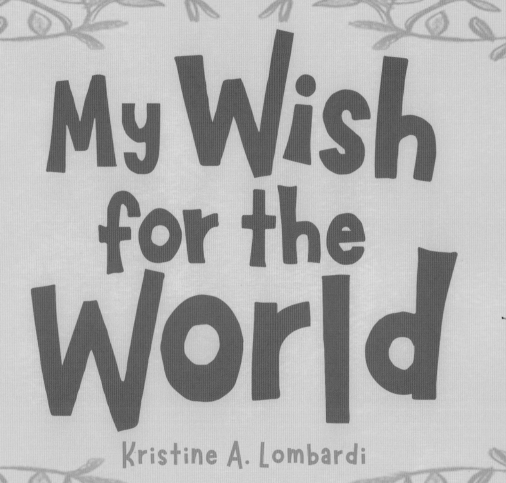

My Wish for the World

Kristine A. Lombardi

Christy Ottaviano Books

LITTLE, BROWN AND COMPANY

New York Boston

About This Book: The illustrations for this book were done in pencil and digitally. This book was edited by Christy Ottaviano and designed by Brenda E. Angelilli. The production was supervised by Lillian Sun, and the production editor was Marisa Finkelstein. The text was set in Marykate, and the display type is Marykate.

• Christy Ottaviano Books • Hachette Book Group • 1290 Avenue of the Americas, New York, NY 10104 • Visit us at LBYR.com • First Edition: March 2023 • Christy Ottaviano Books is an imprint of Little, Brown and Company. • The Christy Ottaviano Books name and logo are trademarks of Hachette Book Group, Inc. • The publisher is not responsible for websites (or their content) that are not owned by the publisher. • Library of Congress Cataloging-in-Publication Data • Names: Lombardi, Kristine A., author, illustrator. • Title: My wish for the world / Kristine A. Lombardi. • Description: First edition. | New York : Christy Ottaviano Books/Little, Brown and Company, 2023. | Audience: Ages 4–8. | Summary: Delivers a hopeful message about all the ways we can wish for kindness in the world around us, such as caring for those who need help. • Identifiers: LCCN 2022002881 | ISBN 9780316433150 (hardcover) • Subjects: CYAC: Stories in rhyme. | Kindness—Fiction. | LCGFT: Picture books. | Stories in rhyme. • Classification: LCC PZ8.3.L84213 My 2023 | DDC [E]—dc23 • LC record available at https://lccn.loc.gov/2022002881 • ISBN 978-0-316-43315-0 • PRINTED IN CHINA • APS • 10 9 8 7 6 5 4 3 2 1

To my sweet mom, who always raised me to be kind, respect the world around me, and love unconditionally

My wish for the world—
there are more than a few.
I wish a much kinder place
for me and for you.

I wish we'd respect nature
and just let it be.

And not take much
from the land or the sea.

I wish we'd think twice about
what we leave behind.
And make time to clean up,
to be courteous and kind.

I wish we'd love all creatures
no matter how small.

And give back to the earth
for the benefit of all.

I wish we'd give shelter
to those in need.

And offer what we no longer use
to help others succeed.

I wish we'd see everyone we meet
as a potential friend.

And look out for one another
so hurting hearts can mend.

I wish we'd take the time to listen
with understanding and grace.

For we are all in this world together—
every being, religion, and race.

This is my wish for the world—
for you and for me.
There's always more we can do
to make it a better place to be.

TIPS TO MAKE THE WORLD BETTER

⭐ Adopt a shelter pet.

⭐ Befriend the new kid in class.

⭐ Make a bird feeder.

⭐ Help someone in need.

⭐ Pick up and discard litter on the ground.

⭐ Start a lemonade stand and donate the money to a charity.

⭐ Share your toys.

⭐ Open the door for someone.

⭐ Turn the faucet off while brushing your teeth.

⭐ Make a card for a friend who might need some cheer.

⭐ Compliment your classmate on a drawing or project.

⭐ Help an older person with shoveling or moving their trash cans to and from the curb.

⭐ Give someone a big hug.